Guatemala
A B C

Written by
Edna Valenzuela

_____

Illustrated by
Melissa Matzir

Libélula / dragonfly

Dedicatoria

Para Camila y Elena
Las amo mis amores.

A es para el **Arco** de Santa Catalina.

is for the Santa Catalina **Arch.**

B es para el **Biotopo** del Quetzal, una reserva natural.

B is for **Biotope** del Quetzal, a nature reserve.

MIRADOR
A 275 mts.

SENDERO
JUAN XOCCAAL

C

es para los granos de **café.**

is for **coffee** beans.

D es para **danta**, también conocido por tapir.

is for **danta**, also known as tapir.

4

E es para el Cristo Negro de **Esquipulas**.

is for the Black Christ of **Esquipulas** (es-kee-poo-las).

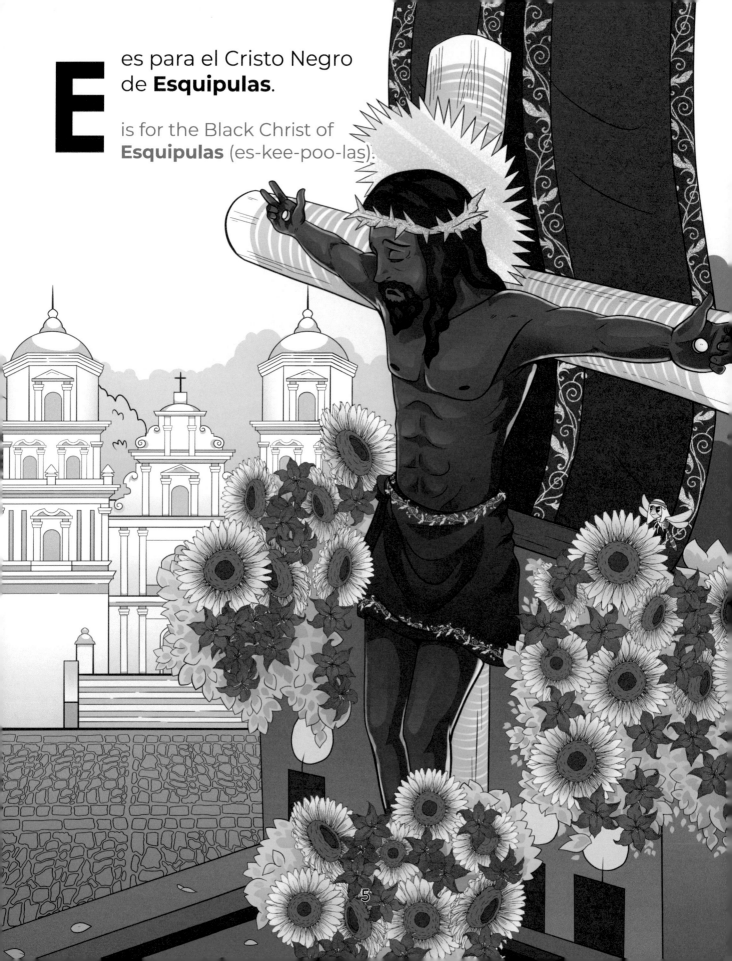

F es para plátanos **fritos**.

is for **fried** plantains.

G es para los barriletes **gigantes** que celebran a los muertos.

is for the **giant** kites that commemorate the dead.

7

es para **huipil**, las blusas bordadas que visten las mujeres indígenas.

is for **huipil** (wee-peel), the embroidered blouse worn by indigenous women.

H

8

es para **iguana**.

is for **iguana**.

9

J es para el Templo del Gran **Jaguar**.

is for the Temple of the Great **Jaguar**.

K es para **Kak'ik**, un caldo hecho con la pierna de chompipe.

is for **Kak'ik**, a stew made with turkey leg.

L es para la **Laguna** de Ixpaco y su lodo rico en minerales.

is for the Ixpaco **Lagoon** and its mineral-rich mud.

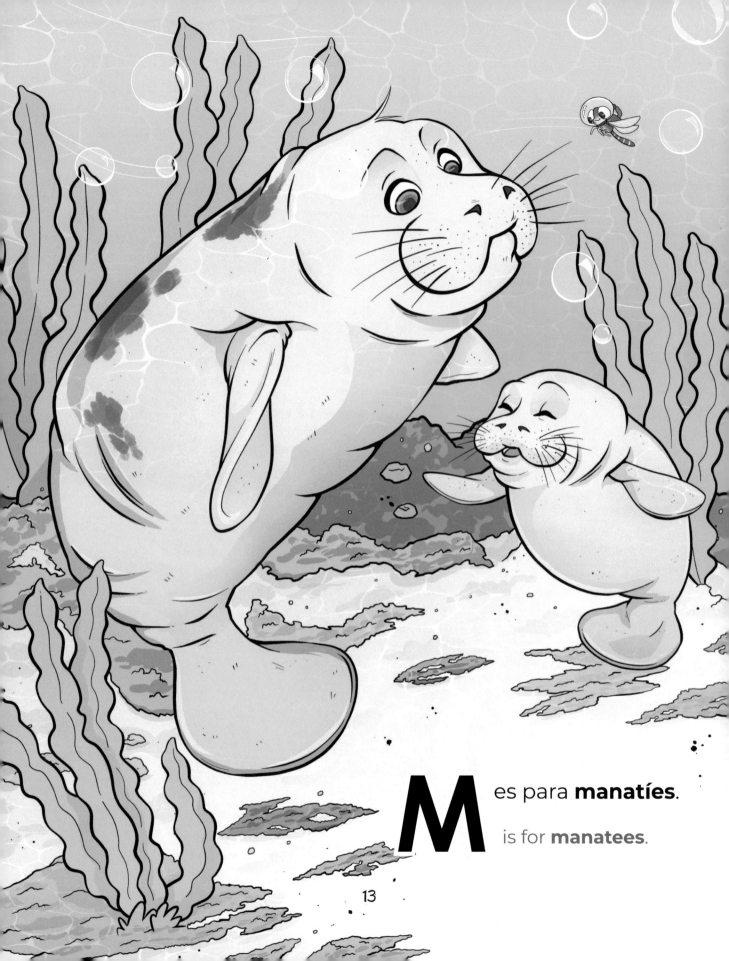

M es para **manatíes**.

is for **manatees**.

N es para la flor **nacional**, la orquídea Monja Blanca.

is for the **national** flower, the White Nun orchid.

O es para los **ornamentos** de cerámica.

is for ceramic **ornaments**.

15

P es para **piñata**.

is for **piñata** (pee-nyah-tah).

16

Q es para las ruinas de **Quiriguá**.

Q is for the ruins of **Quirigua**.

17

R

es para el río Motagua, el más largo del país.

is for the Motagua **River**, the longest one in the country.

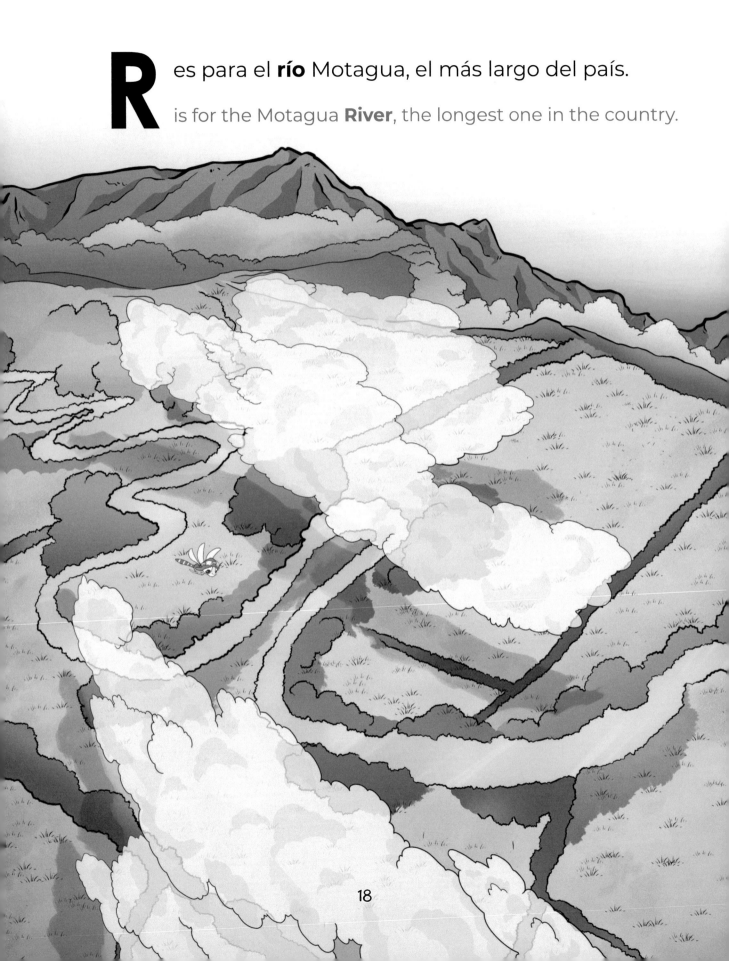

S es para la **serpiente** venenosa el cantil.

is for the venomous cantil **snake**.

T es para los deliciosos **tamales** de elote.

is for the delicious corn **tamales**.

20

U

es para el héroe
Tecún **Umán**.

is for the hero
Tecun **Uman**.

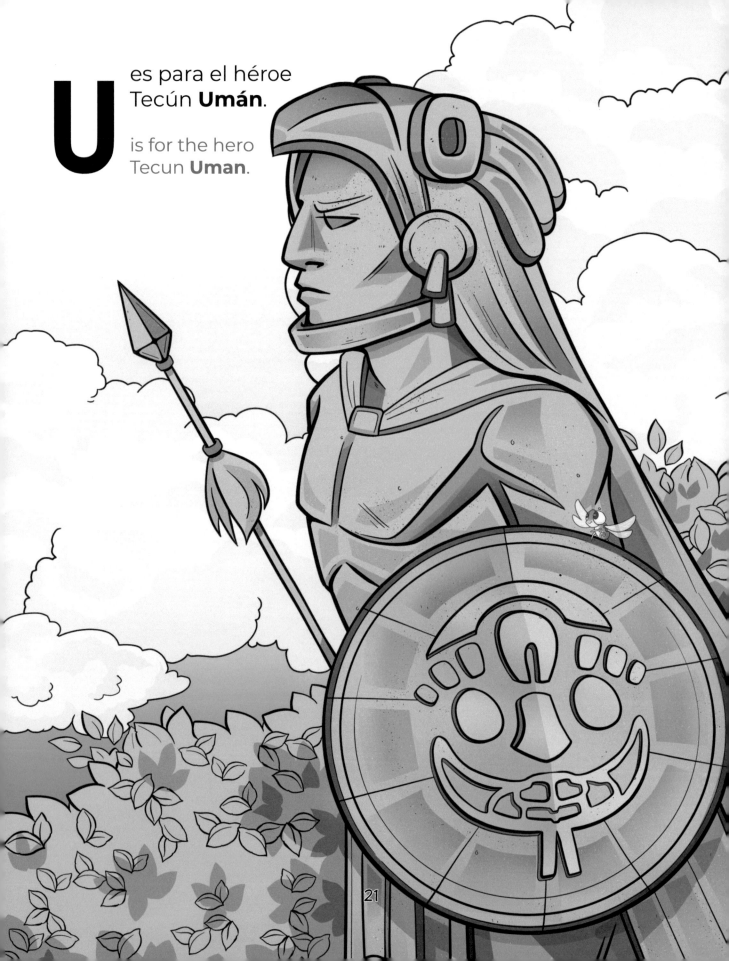

V es para el activo **volcán** Pacaya.

V is for the active Pacaya **Volcano**.

22

W es para **wuj**, que significa libro en K'iche'.

is for **wuj**, which means book in the K'iche' language.

POPOL VUH

23

X es para el pueblo **Xinka**.

is for the **Xinka** people.

24

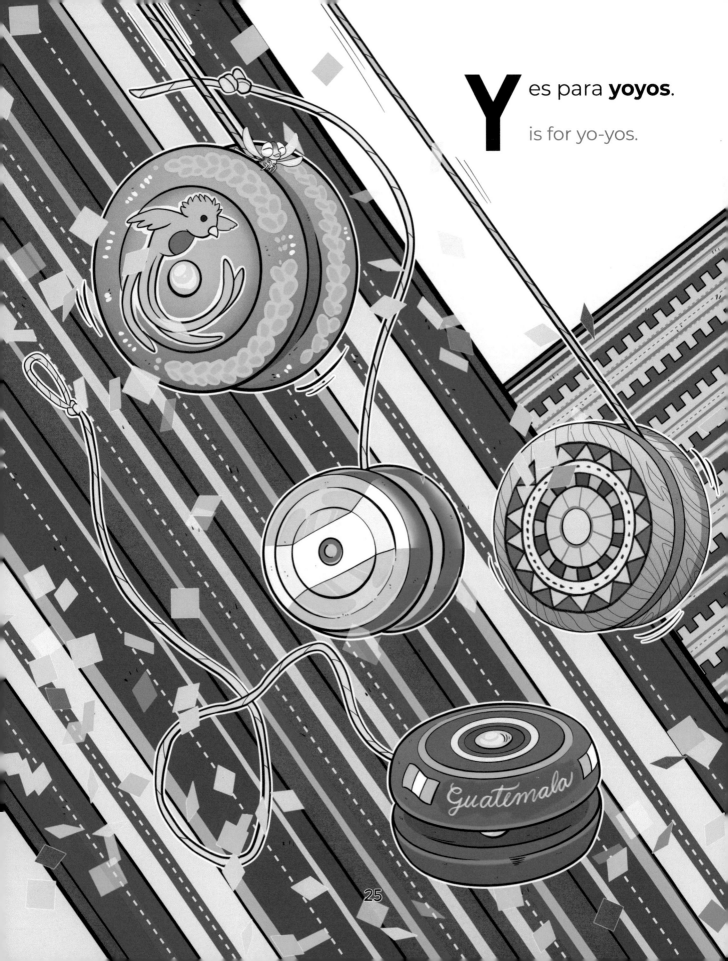

Y es para **yoyos**.

is for yo-yos.

Z es para el parque arqueológico **Zaculeu.**

is for **Zaculeu** Archeological Park.

26

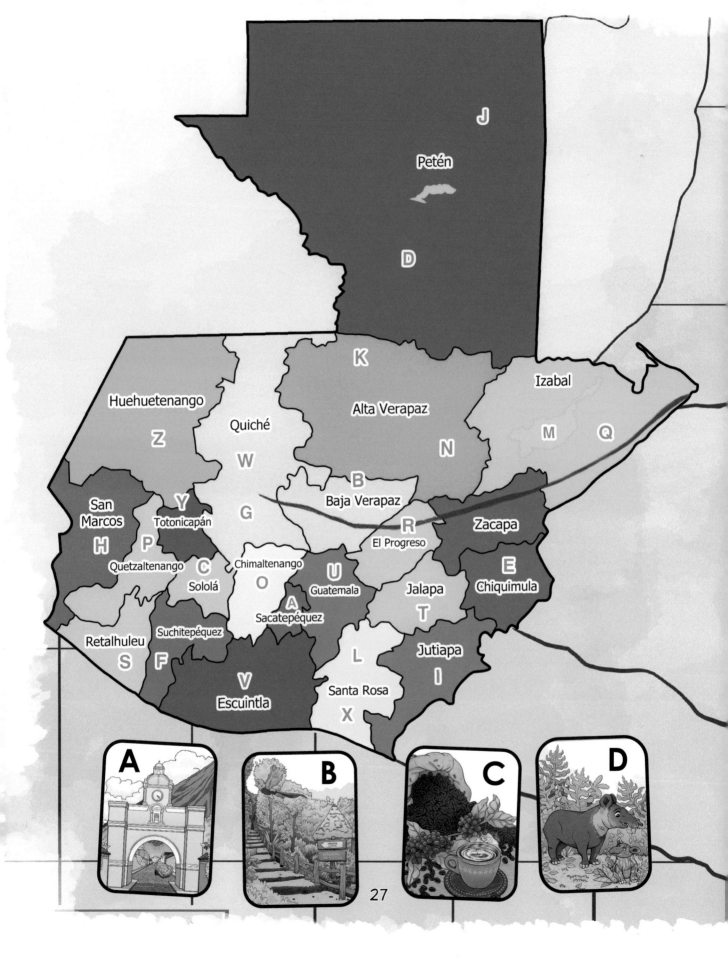

Petén

J

D

K

Huehuetenango

Z

Quiché

W

Alta Verapaz

N

Izabal

M

Q

B

Baja Verapaz

San
Marcos

Y

Totonicapán

G

R

El Progreso

Zacapa

H

P

Quetzaltenango

C

Sololá

Chimaltenango

O

U

Guatemala

A

Sacatepéquez

Jalapa

T

E

Chiquimula

Retalhuleu

Suchitepéquez

S

F

V

Escuintla

L

Santa Rosa

X

Jutiapa

I

27

28

Aa Aa Aa Aa Aa Aa

Bb Bb Bb Bb Bb Bb

Cc Cc Cc Cc Cc Cc

Dd Dd Dd Dd Dd Dd

Ee Ee Ee Ee Ee Ee

Ff Ff Ff Ff Ff Ff

Gg Gg Gg Gg Gg Gg

Hh Hh Hh Hh Hh Hh

I i   Ii   Ii   Ii   Ii   Ii

J j   Jj   Jj   Jj   Jj   Jj

K k   Kk   Kk   Kk   Kk   Kk

L l   Ll   Ll   Ll   Ll   Ll

M m   Mm   Mm   Mm   Mm

N n   Nn   Nn   Nn   Nn

O o   Oo   Oo   Oo   Oo

P p   Pp   Pp   Pp   Pp

Q q   Qq   Qq   Qq   Qq

R r   Rr Rr Rr Rr Rr

S s   Ss Ss Ss Ss Ss

T t   Tt Tt Tt Tt Tt

U u   Uu Uu Uu Uu Uu

V v   Vv Vv Vv Vv Vv

W w   Ww Ww Ww Ww Ww

X x   Xx Xx Xx Xx Xx

Y y   Yy Yy Yy Yy Yy

Z z   Zz Zz Zz Zz Zz

Rellena las letras que faltan y colorea la página.

Fill the missing letters and color the page.